For Mara with all our love
S.H. & H.C.

Text copyright © 1995 by Sarah Hayes
Illustrations copyright © 1995 by Helen Craig

First U.S. edition 1995

Library of Congress Cataloging-in-Publication Data

Hayes, Sarah, 1945–
This is the bear and the bad little girl / by Sarah Hayes ;
illustrated by Helen Craig.—1st U.S. ed.
Summary: When a boy's beloved teddy bear is stolen from a
restaurant by a naughty girl, the boy's dog goes to the rescue.
ISBN 1-56402-648-5 (alk. paper)
[1. Teddy bears—Fiction. 2. Dogs—Fiction. 3. Stories in rhyme.]
I. Craig, Helen, ill. II. Title.
PZ8.3.H324Thb 1995
[E]—dc20   95-10699

2 4 6 8 10 9 7 5 3 1

Printed in Italy

The pictures in this book were done in watercolor and ink.

Candlewick Press
2067 Massachusetts Avenue
Cambridge, Massachusetts 02140

THIS IS THE
BEAR
AND THE
BAD LITTLE GIRL

BY

Sarah Hayes

ILLUSTRATED BY

Helen Craig

CANDLEWICK PRESS
CAMBRIDGE, MASSACHUSETTS

This is the bear
who went out to eat.

This is the dog
left out on the street.

This is the girl
with the curly hair

who said she really
liked the bear.

This is the dog
who put out a paw

and tripped the woman
who came in the door . . .

which pushed the people

waiting to pay . . .

and made the waiter
drop the tray.

This is the boy
all covered in cream

who went to the kitchen
to wash his face clean.

This is the girl
with the curly hair

who said, "You're coming
with me, bear."

This is the girl who
walked down the street

holding the bear
by one of his feet.

This is the dog
who thought it was fun

when the bad little girl
began to run.

This is the girl
who ran faster and faster.

But this is the dog
who ran right past her.

This is the girl
who gave the bear back
and said he was
only a baggy old sack.

This is the boy
who said, "I don't care
if he's saggy or baggy,
he's still *my* bear."